Rookie reader®

Bob's Vacation

Written and illustrated by
Dana Meachen Rau

Children's Press®
A Division of Scholastic Inc.
New York   Toronto   London   Auckland   Sydney
Mexico City   New Delhi   Hong Kong
Danbury, Connecticut

For Chris, who took charge of the move
so I could finish my pictures.
—D. M. R.

Visit Children's Press® on the Internet at:
http://publishing.grolier.com

Reading Consultant
Linda Cornwell
Learning Resource Consultant
Indiana Department of Education

Library of Congress Cataloging-in-Publication Data
Rau, Dana Meachen.
    Bob's vacation / written and illustrated by Dana Meachen Rau.
        p. cm. — (A rookie reader)
    Summary: A snowman becomes bored with snow because it is not colorful enough.
    ISBN 0-516-21543-4 (lib. bdg.)   0-516-26472-9 (pbk.)
    [1. Color—Fiction. 2. Snow—Fiction. 3. Snowmen—Fiction.] I. Title. II. Series.
PZ7.R193975Bm 1999
[E]—dc21   98-19037
                                                                              CIP
                                                                              AC

GROLIER
PUBLISHING
        5 6 7 8 9 10 R 08 07 06 05 04 03 02 01

Bob thought snow was boring.

"Snow is too white!

I need more colors!" he said.

So Bob went on a vacation.

He built castles

with *yellow* sand.

He surfed on **blue** waves.

He climbed up green trees.

13

He rode in **red** boats.

Bob loved all
the bright colors.

But the sun
was too hot.

18

Bob was getting too thin!

So Bob took a trip
back home.

"Let's think of ways to make snow fun!" he said.

Now, Bob builds castles

with *white* snow.

He sleds on **white** hills.

He climbs up **white** icebergs.

He rides on **white** ice floes.

And he always wears *bright colors!*

Word List (67 words)

a	climbed	in	sand	trip
all	climbs	is	sleds	up
always	colors	let's	snow	vacation
and	floes	loved	so	was
back	fun	make	sun	waves
blue	getting	more	surfed	ways
boats	green	need	the	wears
Bob	he	now	thin	went
boring	hills	of	think	white
bright	home	on	thought	with
builds	hot	red	to	yellow
built	I	rides	too	
but	ice	rode	took	
castles	icebergs	said	trees	

About the Author

Steamy hot chocolate, a blazing fireplace, and cozy mittens are some of Dana Rau's favorite wintertime things. But big, sloppy drops of snow are the best—they make perfect snowmen. Dana is the author of many books for children, including *A Box Can Be Many Things* and *The Secret Code* in the Rookie Reader series. *Bob's Vacation* is the first book she has written and illustrated. Dana also works as a children's book editor and builds snowmen with her husband, Chris, in Farmington, Connecticut.